The Blessing Cup

To my daughter, Traci,

and my son, Steven

SIMON & SCHUSTER BOOKS FOR YOUNG READERS · An imprint of Simon & Schuster Children's Publishing Division · 1230 Avenue of the Americas, New York, New York 10020 · Copyright © 2013 by Patricia Polacco · All rights reserved, including the right of reproduction in whole or in part in any form. · SIMON & SCHUSTER BOOKS FOR YOUNG READERS is a trademark of Simon & Schuster, Inc. · For information about special discounts for bulk purchases, please contact Simon & Schuster Special Sales at 1-866-506-1949 or business@simonandschuster.com. · The Simon & Schuster Speakers Bureau can bring authors to your live event. For more information or to book an event, contact the Simon & Schuster Speakers Bureau at 1-866-248-3049 or visit our website at www.simonspeakers.com. · Book design by Laurent Linn · The text for this book is set in Lomba. · The illustrations for this book are rendered in two and six B pencils and acetone markers. · Manufactured in China · 0513 SCP · 10 9 8 7 6 5 4 3 2 1 · Library of Congress Cataloging-in-Publication Data · Polacco, Patricia. · The blessing cup / Patricia Polacco. — 1st ed. · p. cm. · "A Paula Wiseman Book." · Summary: A single china cup from a tea set left behind when Jews were forced to leave Russia helps hold a family together through generations of living in America, reminding them of the most important things in life. · ISBN 978-1-4424-5047-9 (hardcover) — ISBN 978-1-4424-5048-6 (ebook) [1. Drinking cups—Fiction. 2. Jews—Fiction. 3. Family life—Fiction.] I. Title. · PZ7.P75186Ble 2013 · [E]—dc23 · 2012023596

first edition

The Blessing Cup

PATRICIA POLACCO

A Paula Wiseman Book

SIMON & SCHUSTER BOOKS FOR YOUNG READERS

New York   London   Toronto   Sydney   New Delhi

When my great-grandmother Anna was a little girl, long before she came to America, she lived in a small *shtetl* with her mother, papa, and baby sister, Magda, near Tver in Russia.

Life was made harder yet whenever the czar's soldiers came.

"Why do they do this to us, Momma?" Anna cried to her mother.

As her mother rocked Anna and Magda in her arms, she whispered, "I don't know, my child. . . . I don't know."

When it was safe, Anna's mother took them into the kitchen. Soon Anna's papa came home. When they all sat down, Anna's mother placed two candlesticks on the table. She climbed up on the warming stove and pulled down something that was lovingly covered with an embroidered cloth. Underneath was a magnificent china tea set. It was Friday and the sun had set.

Anna's mother lit the candles and whispered prayers that began *Shabbat*. "Tell us again, Momma. . . . Tell us about the tea set," Anna teased.

"Well," her mother began, "it was many years ago, just after your papa and I were married. A horse-drawn cart came to our village all the way from Tver. On it was the biggest wooden crate I had ever seen. Everyone in Roynovka gathered around to see what was in it. That is when I discovered the crate was for me!" she exclaimed with a grand gesture.

"And when I unpacked it, everyone in the village stepped back. It took their breath away. . . . It was this beautiful china tea set that you see before you now!"

"But, Momma . . . The note . . . Tell us about the note again," Anna insisted.

"Inside of this pot was a note. It was from my aunt Rebecca in Minsk. It read, 'Rachel, this is for you to celebrate your marriage. This tea set is magic. Anyone who drinks from it has a blessing from God. They will never know a day of hunger. Their lives will always have flavor. They will know love and joy . . . and they will never be poor!'"

It was true, Anna thought. God had blessed them. Before their evening meals
Momma would always say, "So that our lives will always have flavor." Anna felt nothing
but love and joy in her mother's house. And even though their lives were humble

because there was never enough money, Anna's papa would say to her, "Oh, there is rich and there is rich. *We* are richer than kings, and do you know why?" Then he and Anna chanted together, "Because we have each other!" Anna felt that in Roynovka *everyone* was rich. They had one another!

Winter was coming to an end in Roynovka. The first signs of spring were peeking through the last thin blankets of snow. But it was still cold, so Anna's family slept all together in the warming bed on top of the brick oven in the kitchen.

As Anna drifted off to sleep, she watched the flickering light on the oven make patterns on the tea set. It was as if they were dancing just for her.

Suddenly in the middle of the night Anna was startled awake to terrible sounds.

"What's happening, Momma?" Anna screamed. Her mother bundled Anna and Magda into the goat house, where they hid while Anna's papa ran to the temple.

When her papa got there, it was too late. The temple was in flames. Rabbi Weismantle shook a paper in Anna's papa's face. "The czar has ordered all Jews to leave Russia. . . . All of us . . . ," he sobbed.

"This is happening everywhere in Russia," the commandant of the soldiers called out.

Anna's papa rushed back to his home to tell his family.

For the next days everyone had to sell or give away their meager belongings.
They were ordered to pack what they could drag in carts or carry . . . and leave!

"Where will we go, Momma?" Anna asked.

"Your papa has a cousin in a faraway land called America. . . . Perhaps we can
go there," her mother whispered.

"How far away is it?" Anna asked.

"Across a vast sea. . . . So you must help me now and be brave."

"I don't want to leave," Anna cried softly.

"None of us do," her mother whispered as she packed.

"Why don't they want us here?" Anna finally asked.

"Because we are different from them. . . . They are afraid of what they don't understand," Anna's mother said, wrapping the beautiful tea set in soft clothing.

"It will bring God's blessings with us on our journey," her mother whispered.

Anna's papa loaded his sewing machine, their *menorah*, the *shofar*, his *tallis*, and his holy books. "This is the last of what we are able to take with us," he said, sighing.

He placed Anna and her sister in the cart and he and their mother slowly pulled the cart away.

Anna looked back at her village as long as she could see it. Only when it disappeared from her sight did she look ahead and wonder what their new life in America would be.

That first night they stayed in a cold barn with other refugees fleeing the *pogroms*. Anna's mother went to the well and drew water in the china tea pot, and said, "May God's blessings be upon us." Then she broke bread and sprinkled salt upon it and whispered, "Bread so that we shall never know hunger in our new life. Salt so that our lives will always have flavor. . . . We shall always know love, and as long as we are together we shall never be poor."

Then she passed the cup to each of them. They drank the water, ate their salted bread and raisins, and then hugged close and went to sleep.

As time went on, the journey was very hard. On some nights they were welcomed to sleep in barns. On other nights they were chased away. Most nights Anna's papa slept on the ground while his family slept in the cart. The open ground was damp and he shivered with the cold.

As the months passed, Magda was no longer a baby in her mother's arms. Anna's papa did odd jobs to get enough money as they continued their flight from Russia.

It was a hard fall, and as they approached yet another new town it was getting harder for Anna's papa to pull the cart. Then, on the outskirts, he couldn't take another step. He collapsed. Anna's mother ran to find a doctor. When the doctor arrived, he listened to Papa's chest.

"Your husband is very ill. He needs medicine, good food, rest, warmth, and care!" he said.

Anna's mother looked distressed.

"You can stay with me. . . . I live quite alone now. I'll make your husband well," the doctor said as he brought them into his home.

Anna, Magda, and their mother looked around the doctor's fine house.

"Look at these rugs," Anna's mother said as they all leaned over and felt one of them.

"My late wife collected fine Persian rugs. There's a rich merchant just down the street who has offered me a fortune for that one!" the doctor chirped with a broad smile.

After he put Anna's papa to bed, he came into the kitchen.

"Can you cook, woman? That is the question!" he boomed. Anna's mother smiled back and bowed.

"Such food I'll make for you, Doctor,"
Anna's mother announced, opening
cupboards and seeing what there was in
the house to prepare to eat.

"Then welcome, my dears," the doctor
said softly.

Yevgeni Vladimorovich Pushkin was true to his word. With his constant care, Anna's papa was soon recovering. The doctor saw to it that Anna and her sister were given proper food and fresh milk every day. It was he who noticed that Anna could not see well, so he fitted her with a pair of spectacles. He took great delight in the good food that Anna's mother prepared. He grew very fond of the two children, and the whole family called him Uncle Genya.

Some months later there was a pounding on the door.

Anna's mother knew right away from the look on Uncle Genya's face what the visit was about.

"They have told you that you cannot house Jews, haven't they?" she asked.

Dr. Pushkin nodded yes.

"Then we shall have to leave," Anna's mother said sadly.

"My dear, your husband cannot survive pulling that cart and sleeping in the open air. He is gravely weakened from the pneumonia." He put on his coat and went out the front door.

When Uncle Genya came back, he asked the family to go into the parlor. He pulled a packet of papers from his pocket.

"I have gotten you all traveling papers so that you can cross borders safely. I also bought these tickets for the train that will take you to Verdansk. There I have arranged passage for all of you on a ship that will take you to America," he said quietly.

Anna's papa fell to his knees and tears filled his eyes. "How, Genya . . . how could you have possibly done this? It had to cost you a small fortune!" he cried.

"Only that rug you are kneeling on . . . I sold it!" Genya said with a broad smile.

"But how can we ever repay you?" Anna's mother cried.

That evening Anna's mother unpacked the tea set and brewed rich black chai tea.

"It brings God's blessings . . . and our desire is that a blessing will forever be on you in this house." Then she taught Uncle Genya the ritual of the bread, salt, love, and being richer than a king!

They all rose very early the next morning. Dr. Pushkin drove them to the train himself in his carriage.

When he arrived back home, he was astonished by what he saw on the sideboard in his dining room. It was the exquisite tea set. Next to it was a note.

Anna's mother had written,

Always remember, dear friend. You are the bread that fed us. You are the salt that flavored our lives. You are the love and joy that held us together. Your golden, kind heart makes you rich indeed. . . . You shall never be poor! I am leaving our precious tea set in your good keeping. We kept one cup so that we can still have its blessing among the four of us. It is all that we will need.

And so it was.

Anna and her family traveled across the sea to America. Anna and her family all stood together at the rail and looked up at the Statue of Liberty.

"Papa . . . are the czar's soldiers here too?" Anna asked as she took his hand.

"No, my dearest. . . . Not here. They can't reach us here," he whispered as he squeezed her hand.

They lived for a time in Manhattan on 10th Street. Anna's papa worked in a tailor's shop just down the block from their three-room walk-up.

Every night Anna's mother got out the one remaining cup and shared tea from it with her family. As they drank, they remembered the bread, salt, love, and richness of being together. They also vowed that they would never forget Uncle Genya.

Eventually Anna's mother and papa moved the family from New York to Union City, Michigan. On every family occasion and holiday they drank from the cup and recited its blessings. Anna's parents lived out their days on that little farm, and shortly after her papa's death, Anna received the cup from her mother.

Anna shared the cup and its blessings with her husband and children all the rest of her life. Shortly before her death she gave the cup to her daughter, Carle.

My grandmother Carle and her family named that cup the "Blessing Cup" and shared its blessings.

In 1938 Carle gave the Blessing Cup to my mother, Mary, on her wedding day.

In 1962 my mother gave the Blessing Cup to me on my wedding day.

I kept the Blessing Cup in an honored place in my home. I drank from it with my own two children while teaching them the blessings that it carried. I stored the cup on the top shelf in my china cabinet. I did, at times, wish that I could have more than one cup so that both of my children could take a piece of our history with them when they married.

On October 17, 1989, at 5:04 in the afternoon my home was rocked by one of the strongest earthquakes that the San Francisco Bay Area has experienced since the great quake in 1906.

When I knew that everyone I loved was safe, I walked into the dining room and to my horror saw my china cabinet overturned. Everything in it had been shattered.

I caught my breath. "Oh, God . . . the Blessing Cup!" I sighed.

When I looked down . . . there it was on the floor in the midst of all the shards of broken glass and china.

It had broken exactly in two. As if by design . . . by an unseen force. I thought of my two children and smiled. I picked up the two pieces and held them close to my heart.

At that moment I realized more than any other time that my ancestors were my bread. That the salt and flavor of my life were their stories. That those stories were kept by them so that I would know that I was loved generations before I was born.

How rich I am indeed.

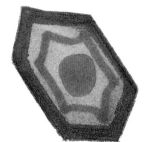